For middles everywhere - A.M.

To Susie and David, with love - N.M.

A Place for Middle
by Angela McAllister & Nick Maland
British Library Cataloguing in Publication Data
A catalogue record of this book is available from
the British Library.
ISBN 0 340 88217 4 (HB)

Text copyright © Angela McAllister 2006
Illustration copyright © Nick Maland 2006

The right of Angela McAllister to be identified as
the author and Nick Maland as the illustrator of this Work has been asserted
by them in accordance with the Copyright, Designs and
Patents Act 1988.

First published 2006
10 9 8 7 6 5 4 3 2 1

Published by Hodder Children's Books
a division of Hodder Headline Limited
338 Euston Road London NW1 3BH

Colour Reproduction by Dot Gradations Ltd, UK
Printed in China

A PLACE FOR MIDDLE

Hodder
Children's
Books

A division of Hodder Headline Limited

Biggest is biggest,

Smallest is smallest.

I'm just in the middle. That's me.

I'm not the fastest,
Or cuddliest,
Or tallest.

Just in the middle.
That's me.

Can't reach,

Can't carry,

Can't work it out.

Just have to try my best.

Can't ask for a clue,
Or a helping hand,
('cause Smallest needs
help from the rest).

Not useful here,

Not useful there,

No use for a Middle like me.

Maybe they just don't need me around.
Where's a place for Middles to be?

I went up and down,

around and   through.

Got hungry for
lunch and all.

I found some lunch,
But it had no middle!
Why, that's no lunch at all!

winding and straight.

Got tired,
and sat on a wall.

Ah, here's a bridge...
But it's got no middle!
Huh! That's no bridge at all!

The sun went in,
The wind blew up,
A storm began to moan.
I fell in a puddle right up to my middle,
Felt soggy and so alone.

Then along came **Biggest** and Smallest and all,
Sad as sad could be.

"There's an empty space right there,"
they said. (Perhaps it might fit me?)

I looked at the space...

It might fit a Middle...

It DID fit a Middle!

"YIPPEE!!!"

"Perfect!" said Biggest and Smallest and all.
"Without a Middle we're no family at all.
That's where a Middle should be!"